D0801543

THE POPCORN SPY

THE POPCORN SPY

MARANKE RINCK

illustrated by **MARTIJN VAN DER LINDEN**

translated by Nancy Forest-Flier

LQ

LEVINE QUERIDO

MONTCLAIR · AMSTERDAM · HOBOKEN

This is an Em Querido book
Published by Levine Querido

LEVINE QUERIDO

www.levinequerido.com · info@levinequerido.com

Levine Querido is distributed by Chronicle Books LLC

Text copyright © 2020 by Maranke Rinck
Illustrations copyright © 2020 by Martijn van der Linden
Translation copyright © 2022 by Nancy Forest-Flier

Originally published in the Netherlands by Querido

Library of Congress Control Number: 2020949892
ISBN 978-1-64614-095-4

Printed and bound in China

Published in September 2021
First Printing

Book design by Patrick Collins
The text type was set in Fresco Normal

Martijn van der Linden drew the illustrations for this book with a 2B pencil
on 300 gsm paper while eating a mix of salty and sweet popcorn.

This publication has been made possible with financial support
from the Dutch Foundation for Literature.

N ederlands
letterenfonds
dutch foundation
for literature

There are lots of seats on the plane.
With passengers in every seat.
Packed in tight.
Like kernels on a corncob.
Farmer Bill groans.

The woman next to him doesn't look up.
She keeps typing on her laptop.
"Good plan, Bill," she says.
"Try flying to Holland on your tractor.
I'll see you when you get there."

Bill doesn't say a word.
He doesn't want to go to Holland.
He doesn't even know where Holland is.
But it's a long way from America, that's
for sure.
It takes them nine hours to get there.

Bill trudges along after the woman.
It's nighttime in America now.
But here in Holland it's already morning.
He yawns.

The woman opens a car door.
"To the hotel," she says.
Bill is about to get in too.
But the woman stops him.
She points to a bike.

The woman smiles.
"That's how it is in Holland," she says.
"Here everyone does everything by bike.
You don't want to stand out, do you, Bill?"
She gives him a stack of papers.
"This is what we know so far.
The name of the girl.
And her address."

6

The woman gets in the car.
She slams the door shut.
The window slides down.
The woman sticks her head out.
"Study the case, Bill.
And tell me all about
it this afternoon.
Come on!
No dillydallying!
Get on that bike,
man!"

Snotty pedals!
How do you work this thing?

ELLIS

CHAPTER 1

CARROT?

My teacher is a carrot.
Mr. Mike is a tomato.
And I'm standing here acting like this is
completely normal.
Like *everything* is completely normal.
But it's not.

There are two secrets in my backpack.
If Ms. Kim found out,
she wouldn't be acting so happy.

We're celebrating that we're officially a
healthy school.
We already were.
But now it says so on a golden sign.
Somebody put his signature on it.
The mayor.
Or the prime minister. Whatever.
They probably eat hamburgers at work
every day.
But we're not allowed to eat any good stuff
at school now.
Some of the
parents are
clapping and
cheering.
Including
my dads.
Unbelievable.

We're not allowed to bring cookies
to school.
No candy, no sugary drinks.
That doesn't bother me so much.
I have only one problem with the school's
new rules.

No popcorn.

I just don't get it.
Ms. Kim thinks popcorn is disgusting.
Even the word makes her shiver.
Sometimes I say it anyway.
Just for fun.

Look at that cloud, Ms. Kim!
It's like a big piece of POPCORN!

Brrrrrr.

Ms. Kim says popcorn is unhealthy.
But it's really not that bad.
Popcorn makes you happy.
How can that be unhealthy?
I'm *never* going to stop eating popcorn.
Even if the king makes it illegal!

I have a bag of popcorn in my backpack
right now.
It's a secret, but not from everyone.
Only the kids in my class know about it.

I have *another* secret.
My biggest secret.
One that nobody knows about.
It's...

Psst. Ellis.
Are you going to eat
that nice juicy carrot?

...Bob.
Popcorn Bob.
The living popcorn kernel.
As big as a kiwi.

Bob is not an easy guy to live with.
He's always hungry.
He never sleeps.
And he's got a really bad temper.
But he's also my very best friend.
Every day we secretly hand out popcorn.
To all my classmates.
Because *every* kid has a right to popcorn!
I can't think about anything else.
Neither can Bob.

Yummy, there's a giant carrot walking around out there!

We have to be careful.
There are too many people around us.
I see Fay looking at me.
I give her a wave.
Then I turn.
My heart is pounding.
I zip my backpack all the way up.
I can't let anybody find out about Bob.
"Hey!" he shouts from inside.
"Where's my little peephole?"
But I can hardly hear him.

CHAPTER 2

"OKAY...NOW!"

Finally the veggie party is over.
Hundreds of kids run inside.
They head for their classrooms, stumbling
over each other.
Just like popcorn falling into a bowl.
I don't do anything.
I wait with my backpack in my hands.
Ms. Kim is already in our classroom.
Nobody notices me.

I only have twenty seconds.
After that I have to be back in my seat.
I quickly open my bag.
"Hurry," I whisper.

Bob hops to his regular lookout spot.
That's where he stands guard.
He's almost invisible.
I pretend to be tying my shoelace.
"Wait a minute,"
Bob whispers.
A kindergartener
rushes by.

I crouch down and scurry to the coatrack.
Then I stuff a handful of popcorn into
each coat pocket.
It's going really well.
I've done almost all of them.
Then Bob hums
our warning call.

Hm hm hm hoo hoo...

I drop my bag.
My right hand is still full of popcorn.
I jump to my feet.
With my hands behind my back.
Somebody's coming!

It's Mr. Mike, our principal.
He's taken off his tomato suit.
But he *is* still
wearing bright
red sneakers.

Hey, Ellis.
What are you
up to?

A few pieces
of popcorn fall
on the floor.
Oh, no.
I have to distract him.
I quickly try to cover the popcorn with
my feet.
"Hey, Mr. Mike," I say.
"You were a really good tomato just now!"
I nod my head up and down.
It sounds crazy, but it works.
"Thank you, Ellis," says Mr. Mike.

"I've always wanted to be a good tomato.
Now hurry back to your class."

I'm nervous for the rest of the day.
It's not because of Bob.
He hasn't stolen any food.
He hasn't run away.
But I feel like I'm being watched.
Much more so today than in the past
few weeks.
Even on the way home, I have this feeling
that someone is following me.
I keep looking around.
Bob starts to complain.
"Hey, you, hold that bag still!"

Bob crawls onto my shoulder.
He likes to sit there.
But I want him off.
"Get back in the bag," I say quietly.
"They can see you up here."
Bob groans.
"Who?"

Do you see anybody?

"In the bag, Bob," I hiss.
Bob does what I say, but he's very grouchy.
For the hundredth time, I turn around.
Bob is right: There's no one there.
The street is empty.

"Dante!" I shout.

"Dante, is that you?"

Dante is the boy next door.

He's probably sneaking up on me.

To scare me or something.

I thought so. There's Louie.

He zooms past.

"Lou!" I shout.

"Where's your brother?"

Suddenly I feel a tap on my shoulder.

CHAPTER 3

DON'T CALL ME "ELLIS-THE-BELLIS"

"Well, if it isn't Ellis-the-Bellis!"
I scowl.
Dante whispers in my ear.

There was no popcorn in my coat today.

I nod.
"BUT WHY
NOT?" he shouts.
He gets this fake-sad look on his face.
"Because you call me 'Ellis-the-Bellis,'" I
tell him.
That's not completely true.
I couldn't put any popcorn in his coat.
I almost got caught.
But Dante doesn't need to know that.

I stick my tongue out at him.
And I run home.
I go around back, into the shed.
And I toss my bag on the floor.
Bob climbs out.

I walk through the yard up to our house.
I'm not worried about Bob.
We're about to make popcorn.
So I'm sure he won't run away.
I open the back door.
"Hi dads, it's me!" I shout.
"I'm going to play outside. Bye!"
I slam the door shut.
There, that takes care of that.

One second later I'm back in the shed.
Where's Bob?
My eyes scan every shelf.
And the floor…
I don't see him.
"Bob?"

Bob keeps throwing newspapers onto
the floor.
He laughs so hard he hiccups.
I shake my head.
I forget to be angry.
Hidden under the newspapers is
the microwave.
I quickly stick a bag of kernels inside.
For three minutes Bob and I do a
popcorn dance.
We count down the last seconds together.
"Five, four, three, two, one…"

I toss the warm popcorn into a bowl.
I sniff.
It smells crazy good.
"Bob," I say.
"Popcorn perfume.
Wouldn't that be a good invention?"
Bob pops a few pieces into his mouth.
"Can you eat perfume?"
I wrinkle up my nose.
Bob rolls his eyes.

Okay. Bad idea.

30

Bob scrambles up to the window.
He peeks outside.
I get ready to hide the popcorn.
"Any fathers out there?" I ask.
They don't know I'm making popcorn
in here.
And I think they forgot all about the
microwave.
Which is fine with me.
"We're good," says Bob.

The coast is clear.

Bob dives back into the popcorn bowl.
That means I have to hurry up, before he
eats it all himself.
Which he could easily do.
"You're just like a piranha," I tell him.
"A what?" Bob asks with his mouth full.
"One of those fish with the pointy teeth,"
I say,
"that can eat a whole cow in two seconds."

"Oh," says Bob.
"Does cow taste good?"

Suddenly the door of the shed flies open.
I scream.

CHAPTER 4

THIS IS AMAZING

There's Dante, standing in the doorway.
I stare at him.
Bob and I do nothing.
Ab-so-lute-ly nothing.
We sit on the floor and we don't move.
As if we were frozen.
It's just a few seconds, but it seems
like forever.
Then Bob starts chewing again, very slowly.
He swallows.
And he puts another piece of popcorn
in his mouth.
Dante points
to him.

Suddenly I can move again.
I jump up.
I grab Dante by his finger and pull him
into the shed.
Then I push the door shut with my foot.
"Dante," I say.
"This is Bob.
Bob…Dante. He lives next door."

Dante's eyes start to glow.
"Wow," he says.
He comes closer, walking very slowly.
"Wowie, wow.
Look at that…
A POTATO MAN!"

Bob puts up his fists.

Listen, kid!
I am BOB.
Popcorn Bob.
Don't call me
a potato!

Dante takes a step back.
He glances up at me.
"He *looks* like a potato.
Is he a kind of robot?
How many batteries does he use?"

Bob scrunches up his eyes.
He starts shaking all over.
"Don't make him angry,"
I say quickly.
But it's too late.

Bob flips out.

I do not look like a potato!

Bob is furious.
And when Bob is
furious, he changes.
Into a big, white piece
of popcorn.
I've seen it happen over and over again.
But this time he does something different.
He doesn't just bounce all
over the place.
He attacks Dante!
He goes for his leg.
Growling like
a wolf.

I've never seen him like this.

"Bob!" I shout.

Bob sinks his teeth into Dante's pants.

And he doesn't let go.

"Whoa!" Dante calls out.

He shakes his leg.

But Bob holds on tight.

"Let go, Bob!" I yell.

And to Dante: "Tell him you're sorry!

Tell him he's not a potato!"

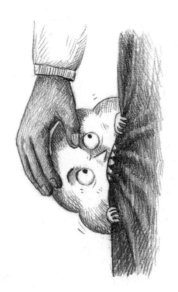

Dante bursts out laughing.
"What?
Okay, okay…I'm sorry!"
Bob stops growling.
Dante touches him. Very carefully.
He strokes his popcorn head.
"You're not a potato," he says.
"I can see that now."

Dante keeps stroking him.
"Be careful," I say.
"Or he'll bite your finger.
He bit my finger at first."

But Bob doesn't bite.
He changes back into a popcorn kernel.
I'm totally blown away.
Bob calmly puts on his hat.
Dante is beaming.
"This is amazing."
He looks at Bob.
"You are amazing!"
Bob nods.
"An amazing...what?"
I hold my breath.
"Popcorn kernel!" Dante shouts.
"An amazing popcorn kernel!"

And your name is Bob! Ha ha! That is awesome!

CHAPTER 5

WHO IS THAT ANYWAY?

I have no choice.
From now on, Dante is one of us.
Well…it could be worse.
Dante has lived next door all my life.
He likes to call me Ellis-the-Bellis.
It makes no sense.
But otherwise he's all right.
"Promise you won't tell anyone about
this," I say.
Dante nods.
"I promise."
I shake my head.

Promise harder.

Dante makes a V with his fingers.
He spits through it onto the floor.
"Ellis-the-Belli…"
I frown.
"My name is *Ellis*."
"Ellis," says Dante solemnly.
"I PROMISE I won't say a word.
Really.
Never."
"Good," I say.
And then I tell him how I made Bob.
That one of my popcorn kernels
didn't pop.
That I put it back in the microwave.

"And, well…ta-da!"

"And you've had him for *two weeks*
already?" asks Dante.
"Why haven't you told me?"
"It's a secret," I say.
"Imagine what would happen if they
saw Bob.
They'd grab him and take him away.
And my popcorn paradise too."
"Popcorn paradise?" asks Dante.
"The shed," I say.
"I can make as much popcorn in here as
I want.
And I have to.
Because I want to keep handing it out to
the kids in our class."

Dante looks at me.
"You're a hero, Ellis."
A kind of Robin Hood.
But with popcorn."
I burst out laughing.
Bob laughs too.
He even rolls on the floor.

"Are you okay?" I ask.
Bob scrambles to his feet.
"Yes, thank you.
I'm fine."

Dante picks Bob up.
"Robin Hood is from a story.
A really famous story.
He lived in England.
He stole money from the rich and gave it
to the poor.
He didn't do what the king said.
But the king was mean, so that was
all right."

I put a new bag of popcorn in the
microwave.
Dante nods at me.
"You're giving stuff to poor kids too.
Kids who aren't allowed to eat popcorn.
You're not obeying the rules either.
Just like Robin Hood."
I push the button.
"Because the rules are wrong.
Popcorn is *not* unhealthy."
"Exactly!" says Dante.

If rules are wrong, they don't count.

The popcorn starts popping.

Dante slaps me on the shoulder.
"I'm going to help you hand out the
popcorn."
I shake my head no.
"No way.
I do that by myself."

"And with Bob, of course," I say quickly.
Dante tilts his head.
"Do you think Robin Hood did
everything alone?
He had a group of friends.
Guys who helped him with everything."
I don't know what to say.
"Want some popcorn?" I finally ask.
I push the bowl under Dante's nose.
"Hey, what about *me?*" Bob complains.
"*You?* You ate almost the whole first bag
by yourself!"

CHAPTER 6

NO POPCORN

We're eating soup.
I quickly empty my bowl.
I've already swiped three sandwiches.
I'll give them to Bob later on.
He's all alone in my room.
And he's probably starving.
So I want to get to him right away.
But then the doorbell rings.
My fathers look at each other.
"A visitor?" asks Gus.
I jump up from the table.
"I'll get it."
I see Bob in the hallway.
"What are you doing here?" I whisper.
"You were supposed to stay in my room."

The doorbell
rings again.

Hungry.

I open the door.
There's a woman standing on the
doorstep.
"Hi," I say.
The woman looks at me.
But she doesn't say anything.
"Dad?" I call.
The woman keeps staring at me.
It gives me goose bumps.
Then I hear footsteps behind me.
"Hello," says Steve.
"What can I do for you?"
Now the woman starts talking.
But I can't understand a word she says.
She's speaking English.

Dad pushes me gently aside.
"Leave this to me."
I walk up the stairs.
Oh, for crying out loud!
"Why are you still
out here?"
I whisper.
I pick Bob up.
We sit down on
the top step.
That way we're
invisible.
But we can
hear almost
everything.
"They're speaking
English," I whisper
to Bob.
"Can you understand them?"
"Just listen," says Bob.

50

"They're talking about America,"
he whispers back.
"And about popcorn.
That I can understand."

So I can speak English.

Bob looks very proud of himself.
"Good for you," I tell him.
"What else did she say?"
"No idea," says Bob.
"I only heard the word popcorn.
And now I'm even more hungry."
I nod.
So Bob *can't* speak English.
He jabs me in the leg.
"HUNGRY, Ellis. Did you hear me?"

Are you going to make
me some popcorn?

The front door closes.
I quickly fish a sandwich out of my bag.
"Here," I whisper.
"Stay up here, Bob."
Then I run downstairs.
"What was *that* all about?"
Steve shrugs his shoulders.
"No idea.
It was an American lady.
She wanted popcorn."
Gus bursts out laughing.

Steve nods.
"She said, 'Give me the popcorn.'
So I said:

Madam, we only eat healthy food.
We have no popcorn here.
Good evening!

Chuckling, my
fathers clear
the table.

I don't laugh.
That woman.
She asked for
our popcorn.
Does she...
Does she know
something about Bob?
I shake my head.
No, that's impossible.

CHAPTER 7

WHAT FUN

I want to talk to Dante.
But Louie is coming to school with us.
So I have to be patient.
Until recess.
Then I'll tell him about that woman from
yesterday.
"What fun," says Dante.
"All FOUR OF US going to school together."
He winks at me.
He knows that Bob is in my backpack.
"Tigers don't have fun,"
says Louie.
He shoots ahead on
his scooter.

> Tigers like to be alone!

I'm glad I'm not a tiger.

At school I wait until everyone is in the
classroom.
Then I quickly stuff handfuls of popcorn
into the coats and bags.
After that Bob begs to come with me
instead of staying in my bag.

"Okay, okay," I say.
I sneak him into the class.
And hide him in my drawer.

Ms. Kim holds her hand up.
As if it were a little bowl.
"Something serious has happened,"
she says.
The chattering in the class stops.
Bob pushes my drawer open a tiny bit.

Are you in trouble?

I shut the drawer.
I should have left him in the hall.
The class is so quiet you can hear
a pin drop.
Ms. Kim turns her hand over.
She lets something fall onto the table.
Is it crumbs?
It looks like...

"POPCORN!" says Ms. Kim angrily.
She shivers.
"In the hallway of our HEALTHY
SCHOOL.
Under YOUR coatrack.
It's VERY strange.
Dirty bits of greasy pop…"
I hear Bob moving around in my drawer.
Don't get angry, I say to Bob in my head.

My eyes wander through the classroom.
Are they going to give me away?
Tell the teacher that every day I hand out
popcorn?
Hasna picks at her fingernails.
Emma stares out the window.

Nick and Ted look innocently at the
teacher.
Even Fay doesn't say a word.
But Dante raises his hand.

The teacher looks at him.
She screws up her eyes.
"Was it *your* popcorn?"
Dante shakes his head and points to me.
"I didn't think so," the teacher mutters.

My eyes get big.
My cheeks get hot.
My ears start ringing.

TRAITOR! I roar to myself.
And I keep my drawer shut extra-tight.

CHAPTER 8

I'M SUPER GOOD WITH BUMBLEBEES

The whole class looks at me.
Ms. Kim walks up to my desk.
I can almost see steam coming out
of her ears.
"No, no," shouts Dante quickly.
"I didn't mean THAT!
What I wanted to say is…"

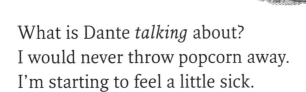

Ellis wanted to help throw the popcorn AWAY!

The teacher stands still.

What is Dante *talking* about?
I would never throw popcorn away.
I'm starting to feel a little sick.

"It was a little girl from the first grade,"
says Dante.
"It was her birthday yesterday.
And...uh...she brought popcorn.
As a treat for the class."
The teacher puts her hand over her mouth.
Dante gives her a little smile.
And he goes on.
"Well, Ellis saw the girl.
And she told her that popcorn isn't
allowed."

Popcorn isn't allowed.

"And then she helped her throw it away.
All of it, right into the garbage can.
I saw it myself.
That's where those crumbs probably
came from."

"Wait a minute," says Emma.
She turns to me.
"Did you throw ALL that popcorn away?"
I don't know what to say.
My stomach is in a knot.
But Dante nods cheerfully.
Hasna frowns.
"How sad for that little girl!
What was she supposed to hand out for
her birthday?"
Dante shrugs his shoulders.
"Empty cups?"

The teacher nods slowly.
"Empty cups," she repeats.
She walks back to her desk.
"Handy.
You can use them to drink tap water.
That's a very healthy way to celebrate.
Good idea, Ellis!
How great that the problem is solved."

All right. Everybody take out your notebooks. Let's have fun with numbers.

The sick feeling is gone.
I open my drawer just a little.
Bob stares out at me through the crack.
"Is that true?" he whispers angrily.

Did you throw POPCORN away?

Oh, no.
He's exploding!

"Raaaah!" roars Bob.
He shoots into the air like a rocket.

My drawer falls on the floor.
It makes a terrible noise.
All my stuff goes flying through the
classroom.
I jump up.
Dante jumps up.

And so does the rest of the class.
Chairs get knocked over.
"What's going on?" shouts the teacher.
"Everybody sit down!"
"I think it's a bumblebee!" shouts Dante.
"I'll catch him."

"No, let me do it!" I scream.
"I'm super good with bumblebees!"
I catch Bob in midair with both hands.
Dante opens the classroom door.
And before anyone can say anything,
we run outside.

CHAPTER 9

THE PRINCIPAL SCORES

We run to the gym.
And disappear into the
locker room.
Luckily there's no gym today.
"Ouch!" I scream.
I stamp my feet and let go of Bob.
"Don't BITE!"
Bob jumps up and down on
the bench.
He rants and rages.
Dante looks at him with eyes
like saucers.
"You're really good at getting
mad, aren't you?
How about running a few
laps instead?
It'll help you cool off."

It's a miracle, but
Bob listens.
He races onto the
gym floor.
Then he starts
running around in
circles and bellowing.
He pounds the air
with his fists.
It's like a weird
boxing match.
After a while he
runs slower.
And slower.
His fists hang lower
and lower.
Then he falls on
the floor.

Dante and I flop down beside him.
And I explain what happened.
"Of course I didn't throw any
popcorn away."

Really?

"No!" I exclaim.
"I'd never do that.
You shouldn't get mad so quickly, Bob!"

Suddenly Dante puts a finger to his lips.
"Shh."
We hear a voice.
Quick as lightning we find a place to hide.
Way in the back of the gym.
Between the vaulting horse and the
trampoline.
A door opens on the other side.

Mr. Mike walks in.

"Yes," he says into his phone.

"Of course all the children will take part.
Hm, hm, yes, yes.
We'll keep a good eye on them.
We'll check all the coats and bags.
Fine, and their shoes too.
I'll discuss it with the team this
afternoon."

Goodbye. See you tomorrow.

He puts his phone in his pocket.
Then he picks up a basketball and shoots.
He misses.

He picks up the ball and
dribbles around a bit.
Then he stands almost
under the basket.
He shoots and he cheers.

WHOA!
AND THE PRINCIPAL SCORES!
WHAT TALENT!
THE CROWD GOES WILD!
AAAAH!

We wait until the principal is gone.
"What are they going to check?" I whisper.
Dante looks worried.
"That's what we're going to find out,"
he says.
"But we have to go back to class now.
Otherwise they'll wonder where we are."

In the class everything is back to normal.
Even my drawer is back under my desk.
I tell the teacher that we let the bumblebee go.
"Good," says Ms. Kim.
And she goes on with the lesson.

Soon it's time for recess.
Bob goes into my coat pocket and comes
outside with me.
Dante eats apple slices.
Every now and then he stuffs a piece into
my pocket.
"Listen," I tell him.
"Yesterday this woman came to our door…"
But something startles me.
"Wait a minute, don't look now,
But Fay is spying on me."

Dante looks straight at Fay.
I turn my back to her.
"DON'T look, I said.
I don't trust her.
Do you think she would tell on me?"
"What do you mean?" asks Dante softly.
"That you're handing out popcorn?
Or do you think she's seen Bob?"
I take my coat off.

There only one way
to find out.

CHAPTER 10

BAD FURRY ELF

Fay is sitting on a bench with Lily.
Next to them is a pile of coats.
I walk up to them.
"Wow!" I say out loud.
"It sure is hot.
Don't you think so, Fay?"
She gives me a dirty look.
I toss my coat onto the pile.
I hope Bob stays put.

Dante and I are
hanging from
the jungle gym.
I tell him
more about
yesterday.

"The woman spoke English," I say.
"And she wanted our popcorn.
Do you think that maybe...
...she's from the popcorn factory?
The American factory where Bob comes
from?"
Dante laughs.
"What gives you that idea?"
I poke him.
Why doesn't he believe me?

"I sent the factory an e-mail," I explain.
"A while ago.
When I had just made Bob.
They wrote back.
They told me to put him in a box and mail
him to the factory.
Of course I didn't
do that."
Dante frowns.
"And you think
that woman
knows something
about Bob?
And that she's
come to get him?
By just knocking
on your door?"
I shrug my shoulders.
I know it sounds crazy.
Maybe I'm seeing things that aren't there.

"The bell's about to ring," says Dante.
We jump off the jungle gym.
I grab my coat from the bench.
"It's a little cold, actually," I mutter.
Fay rolls her eyes.
I feel around in my coat pocket.
Good: Bob's still there.
We run to the bike rack.
No one in sight.
So I take Bob out of my pocket.
"Did it work?" Dante asks him.
"Of course," Bob says.

I understood everything they said.

"Let's hear it," I say.

Bob motions for us to come closer.

"They were talking about a bad furry elf."

Dante gives Bob a tangerine.

The peels go flying in all directions.

"Bob," I say.

"An elf. That's crazy."

Dante chuckles.

"I think they said something that sounds like that.

Furry elf, furry elf.

What could it be?

Maybe...furry shelf?

Or: for yourself?"

"For your health!" I shout.

"You must have heard them say *bad for your health*.

Not *bad furry elf*."

"Maybe," says Bob.

"Bad for your health," says Dante.
"You see.
They were talking about the healthy
school.
What else did they say?"
Bob swallows another piece of tangerine.
"They thought popcorn was a bad
furry elf."
"Bad for your health," I mutter.
Bob nods.

They want to tell the teacher.
That we hand out popcorn.

I squeeze my eyes shut.
They're going to tell on us!
"And you?" I ask.
"Do they know about you?"

Bob shakes his head.
He doesn't think Fay saw him.
That makes it a bit less awful.
But our popcorn secret is still in danger!

The bell rings.
Time to go back to the classroom.
We run after the other kids.
"Fay has to be stopped," says Dante.
"We have to keep her away from
the teacher."
But how are we going to do that?

CHAPTER 11

EVERYTHING OKAY?

Sometimes problems solve themselves.
The teacher isn't in the classroom.
Mr. Osman is leaning over her desk.
"Ms. Kim is with Mr. Mike," he says.
"Making preparations.
For the meeting this afternoon.
They have some *wild* plans."

So I can read to you for a nice long time.

Bob sits in my pocket, nice and quiet.
I guess he likes to be read to.
I wish I had known.

I always stay at school during lunch hour.
But today I'm going to Dante's.
Louie is at a friend's house.
Nobody else is home.
So Bob can run around as much as
he wants.
But he doesn't.
He doesn't do anything at all!
He just lies there on the couch.
Like a floppy doll.
"He can be so cute when he wants to be,"
says Dante.
He strokes his cheek.
"Are you tired, Bob?"
"Do you want to sleep?"

I snatch Bob from the couch.
And I run to the kitchen.
"Bob never sleeps!" I shout.

Do you guys have a microwave?

Dante follows me.
He points to a cabinet.
"In there.
But I'm not allowed to make popcorn."
"I'm not going to," I say.
And I put Bob in the microwave.

Dante wrinkles up his nose.
"Ellis, that can't be good for him.
Bob is alive, right?
Have you ever put an egg in the
microwave?
It explodes!"
I shake my head.
"I hope Bob can't hear you.
He is not an EGG.
He's a kernel of corn.
Sometimes he has to go back in.
It peps him up."
Ping! says the microwave.
I open the door.

"Hello!" says Bob cheerfully.

Everything okay?
What's for lunch?

I have an idea," says Dante.

An idea for lunch?

"First we have to feed him," I say.
"Otherwise we really have problems."

Bob takes a bite of a cheese sandwich.
"So there are two dangers," I say.
"Danger number 1: Fay wants to tell on us."
"Don't worry," says Dante.
"I told you I had an idea, right?
Leave Fay to me."
"What do you have in mind?" I ask.
"Are you going to enchant her with
your smile?"
"Exactly," says Dante.
"Oh!" shouts Bob.

Enchant me
with your
smile too.

Dante grins at him.
Bob giggles.

"I'm going to draw something for Fay,"
says Dante.
"What?" I ask.
Dante can draw really well.
But that's not going to stop Fay from
telling on us, is it?
"She wants me to draw a unicorn for her,"
says Dante.
"She's always asking me.
So I'll draw her a unicorn.

She'll say:

Oh, Dante!
Is that unicorn
for me?

And I'll say:

Yes, but you have to keep your
mouth shut about the popcorn.

And that's that.
Believe me, Fay is no problem."

I look at Robin Hood on the wall.
Maybe it's not so bad after all.
Not having to do everything yourself,
I mean.
"Good," I say.
"But we still have danger number 2.
The teachers.
They have plans for the school.
They're going to check our bags.
Even our shoes.
That's what Mr. Mike said, right?
So we have to find out what they're going
to do.
And that's something *I* have an idea for."

I nod at Bob.

CHAPTER 12

A BALD KIWI

Bob's eyes twinkle.
His skin glistens.
He throws up his arms.
"YESSS.
I'm going to
be a SPY!"

Bob, the Popcorn Spy!

"First you have to hide," I tell him.
"In the teachers' room, when they're
having their meeting.
And then listen in on them.
Just like you did this morning in my coat.
And then tell us everything they said."

"Yeah, yeah, okay," says Bob.
"But more important than that:
WHAT AM I GOING TO WEAR?"

"I shouldn't stand
out," Bob mutters.
"I should be in
the room.

But at the same time
not be in the room.
Like a fly on
the wall."

"Well," says Dante.
"You don't really look like a fly, Bob.
I think it would be better if you went
as a kiwi."

Bob stares at Dante.
"As a WHAT?"

"As a kiwi," says
Dante again.
"Then you can lie in the fruit bowl.
And you can hear everything they say."
Bob looks even angrier.

I shake my head.
Dante looks at me.
"Now what's wrong?
He does look like a bald kiwi, doesn't he?"

Bob explodes.

And at that very
minute we hear a voice.
"Dante!"
Someone's running
up the stairs.

"My mother," says Dante.
"Quick!"
I grab Bob.
"Can you lock the door?" I ask.
But it's too late.
The door swings open.

"Dante, sweetie," says his mother.

You're still here!

Dante's mother speaks Dutch.
But she comes from America.
You can tell by the way she talks.
It sounds funny.
She *is* very nice.
But I'm sitting here with Bob on my lap.
So I'm not really happy to see her.
Oh, no.
She's looking right at me.

"And Ellis is here too," says Dante's
mother.
"How nice!"
I try to smile.
Dante's mother looks around the room.
"You've already eaten, I see?"
Her eyes run over the scraps of food.
When they get to Bob they stop.
He's still a big piece of popcorn.
I'm holding him with two hands.
He's shivering a little.
But otherwise he doesn't move.
"This is my stuffed popcorn doll,"
I tell her.

I press Popcorn Bob against my cheek.
Don't bite me, don't bite me, I think
to myself.
"How sweet, so cute," says Dante's
mother.
"Popcorn with legs."
I try to smile.
"Isn't he?"

Really cute.

I can't get used to the idea.
People don't really *see* Bob.
Even when they *do* see him.
I can say he's a bumblebee.
Or a stuffed animal.
And they believe it!
If I say he's a kiwi later on, will that work?

"It's almost one o'clock," says Dante's
mother.
"Time to go back to school."
Then she babbles something in English.
She sounds just like the woman from
yesterday.
I can't understand a word she says.
But Dante obviously can.
He answers her.
I look at him in surprise.

Since when can
you speak English?

"Since forever," says Dante.
His mother laughs.
"That's what you get with an American
mother.
Now...come on, let's get a move on!"

CHAPTER 13

A SPY WITH
A BAD TEMPER

On the way to school I let Bob sit on my
shoulder.

That cheers him up.

"Those tantrums are a problem," says
Dante.

I sigh.

"A spy with a bad temper.
Not exactly helpful."

"Hey, now YOU GUYS are making me
angry," says Bob.

Dante nods.

"Louie has that sometimes.

My mother tells him to count to ten.

Maybe you could try that, Bob."

1, 2, 3, 4, 5, 6, 7, 8 . . .

"Not NOW," I tell him.

"Only when you think you're getting angry."

"I thought so," Bob mutters.

"What a stupid idea."

We have Mr. Osman for the whole
afternoon.
When it's almost three o'clock, Dante and
I slip into the hall.
I pull Bob out of my bag.
We take him to the bathroom.
Dante takes a few felt-tips out of
his pocket.
He starts to draw.
Bob wriggles and squirms.
"Sit still," I tell him.

But it tickles!

In no time at all Bob is a kiwi.
He looks exactly like one.

The bell rings.
There are lots of kids in the hall.
So no one notices us.
The teachers' room is empty.
I put Bob in the fruit bowl.
My hand is shaking a little.
I just hope he doesn't eat the rest of
the fruit…
Luckily he doesn't.
He keeps turning around until he finds a
comfortable spot.
Just like a cat on your lap.
Then he stops between a banana and
a pear.
He's perfectly still.

The meeting starts.
Dante and I are hanging around in
the hall.
Every now and then we peek inside.
Bob is lying in the
fruit bowl.
He's invisible.

Suddenly we hear applause.
I peek into the teachers' room once again.
Why does everyone look so happy?
"You should see Ms. Kim," I whisper.
"She looks like she's won a prize."

"What do you think they're up to?" Dante murmurs.

I make a guess. "Backpack checks every morning?"

"Yeah, not lice checks but popcorn checks," says Dante.

"Ellis, if that's true..."

I nod.

"Then I can't bring popcorn anymore."

I sigh.

"Just as long as they don't say anything bad about popcorn. If they do, Bob will explode in the fruit bowl."

Now I'm worried. I take another peek through the window.

Ms. Mona stands up.
"Dante, look," I whisper.
The teacher leans over the fruit bowl.
We stare through the window.
Cold sweat starts running down my neck.
Ms. Mona's hand is suspended in the air.
She can't make up her mind.
"Take a pear," Dante whispers.

Ms. Mona takes a pear.

I can breathe again.
That was TOO exciting.

Soon the meeting is over.
We hide until everyone is gone.
Then I take Bob out of the fruit bowl.
"You were a *terrific* spy," I tell him.
"I have news," says Bob.

CHAPTER 14

A MAN WITH
A GOATEE

We walk out of the school.
"Okay, let's hear it, Bob," I say.
He sticks his head out of my bag.

Hungry.

I sigh.
"Please, not now."
"But that fruit smelled *so*
good!" he whines.
He climbs onto my shoulder.
Dante gives him an apple.
"Good," I say.
"You eat your apple.
And in the meantime we'll walk to the
park.
We can have a nice quiet talk there.
But you have to
tell us *everything*!"

On the sidewalk is a man with a goatee.
He's leaning against a bike.
He watches us as we walk past.
I cover Bob with my hair.
That way no one can see him.
But it must tickle.
Because it makes Bob sneeze.
His apple rolls across the sidewalk.
When I look up, the man is still staring
at us.

There are plenty of quiet places in the park.
We plop down under a tree.
Bob dives onto the moss.
"Tell us," says Dante.
"What did you find out?"
He jumps through the grass like a grasshopper.
"Bob," I say sternly.
But he just keeps on jumping.

"Come on, Bob!" I say.
"Tell us what you heard.
What are the teachers planning to do?"

Now Bob stands in front of us with his
legs wide apart.
He takes a blade of grass out of his mouth.
"Okay, I'll tell you,"
he says.

And now he does a handstand.
Dante and I look at each other.
"A movie?" we ask.
"Yes," says Bob, still standing on his head.
"Tomorrow is field day, right?
Well, somebody is coming to make
a movie.
About your healthy school.
Nothing to worry about."

"And that thing about the bags?" I ask.
"They were going to check them?"
"Of course not," says Bob.
"You're not supposed to bring your
backpacks tomorrow.
And you have to wear good shoes.
That's all."

I flop backward onto the grass.
And look up at the popcorn clouds floating
by.
I'm so relieved that I don't see it coming…
Someone is running up to us.
As fast as a jaguar.

I scramble up.
Standing in front of us is the man with
the goatee.
Without his bike.
He acts as if Dante and I aren't there.

He only looks at Bob.
Dante is faster than I am.
He pulls Bob out of the grass.
And sticks him under his shirt.
I'm really, really scared.

Is the man going to steal Bob?
He's much bigger than we are.

I stand up in front of Dante.
"GO AWAY," I scream at the man.
"GO AWAY, YOU!"
I wave my arms.
My voice is trembling.
But it works.
The man hesitates for a second.
Then he turns around.
And runs away.

CHAPTER 15

THE BIG HOTEL

"Who WAS that?" Dante asks.
My throat is shut tight.
"I've seen him before," I squeak.
Dante looks at me with surprise.
"Where?"
Bob's head pops out of Dante's shirt.

Hello.

"Listen to your
Popcorn Spy,
would you?
I don't think this is
the time to stand
around and chat.
Shouldn't we follow that man?"
I nod.
Bob is right.
We have to find out who he is.

I put Bob in my coat pocket.
We run straight through the park.
Bob hates jiggling.
But he doesn't complain.
Suddenly I recognize a figure in the
distance.
"There!" I shout.
The man with the goatee grabs his bike.
He rides away, wobbling back and forth.

"Follow him!" cries Bob.

We chase the man.
Luckily he doesn't bike very fast.
He's really clumsy.
We can easily keep up with him.
Soon we're out of the park.
We cross a road.
The man bikes onto the sidewalk.
But he doesn't put on his brakes!
He slams right into a wall.
Then he gets off.
He's so clumsy that he almost steps on a little dog.
"How mean," I say.

Oof.

Suddenly the man kneels down.
He pets the dog.

The dog's mistress smiles at him.
And the man smiles back.
He says something to her.
It sounds really friendly.
I pick up one word.
"Dante, did you hear that?
He said: America."

Dante nods.
"That man is an American.
You can tell by the way he talks.
Look."

The man goes into the building.
"He's staying here, in the Big Hotel."

"What do we do now?" Dante asks.
"I have to go home," I tell him.
"And make popcorn.
Then I can think better."

"But we'll come back tomorrow.
Then we'll start investigating."
"Tomorrow is field day," says Dante.
I shrug my shoulders.
"Then we'll do it afterward."

CHAPTER 16

IT'S GOING TO BE FUN

That night I can't sleep.
I'm worried.
And Bob is smacking his lips.
We've eaten all the popcorn.
And now he's working on a bag of peanuts
in the shell.
Crack, smack, crack, smack.
"*Shhhhh*," I hiss.
I cover my head with my pillow.

BIP. BIP. BIP.

Growling,
I pull the
pillow away.

Then I crack open a peanut.
"Aren't you worried?" I ask.
Bob calmly goes on eating.
"What about?"
"That someone will discover you," I say.
Bob gives me another peanut.
"I belong with you," he says.

If someone takes me away, I'll bite him on the nose.

And then I'll run straight back to you.

It's almost morning.
I've been lying awake all night, thinking.
About the woman who wants our popcorn.
About the man with the goatee.
Both Americans.
That can't be a coincidence, can it?
They're from the popcorn factory!
Both of them, there's no other
explanation.
If only it was seven o'clock.
I *have* to talk to Dante.

I'm sitting at the breakfast table, yawning.
My fathers are talking about their work.
I grab some toast and grapes from
the table.
And I take a little bite.
Then I stuff the rest into my pockets.
"Excited about field day?" Steve asks out
of the blue.

I start choking.
Then I murmur, "Yeah, sure."
Bob hates it when I run.
He doesn't like jiggling.
I hope I can take it easy.
"So nice to go to the woods with your
class," says Gus.

"Quite a change from having field day on a sports field.
ForestPower is a great sports club.
We did some work for them once, didn't we, Steve?"
Dad nods.
"We had to make sport-theme rubber duckies for them.
A whole series."

A mountain-climbing rubber ducky.

A workout rubber ducky.

A marathon rubber ducky.

I chuckle.
All the kids in my class have normal parents.
My parents design rubber duckies.

Soon we're sitting in the car.
It's a long ride to the woods by bike, so
Gus is driving us.
I whisper to Dante what I was thinking
about last night.
This time he doesn't laugh at me.
He seems worried.
Dad looks at us in the rearview mirror.

"How serious you both look," he says.
"It's too bad about the rain.
But I'm sure it's going to be fun."

I nod absently.
Then I see something in the mirror.
Someone is biking behind our car.
I recognize him right away.
I give Dante a nudge.
"There he is again!"
Dante opens his window.
He sticks his head out.
"You'll get wet that way, Dante," says Dad.
I turn around.
The man has pulled over to the side of
the road.
Rain is pouring down on his hat.
He watches us until we turn a corner.

CHAPTER 17

WEAK OR STRONG?

My father drops us off at the parking lot.
The rain has stopped.
A watery sun is shining.

Dante and I walk over to Ms. Kim.
There's a woman standing next to her.
She has long red hair.
She's holding a stick.
At the end of the stick is a camera.
She's talking to the teacher and looking
through the lens.
Ms. Kim does the same thing.
Mr. Mike claps his hands.
"Everybody come over here!" he shouts.
"Time to count heads."

Our whole class is there.
Mr. Mike points to a man.
"That's Ziggy, our leader.
We do WHATEVER he says."
Ziggy takes one step forward.
"Hi, boys and girls," he roars.
"We're going to have a contest.
We'll be running into ALL KINDS
OF THINGS in the woods.
Bridges, ropes, car
tires, nets.
And mud. Lots and
lots of mud."

The most important thing
is: Just keep going!

I raise my eyebrows.
How am I going to do this
with Bob?
Right now he's sitting
peacefully in my fanny pack.
But will he stay that way?

"Are you guys weak or strong?" yells Ziggy.
"Strong," all the kids mumble around me.
"I SAID: ARE YOU GUYS WEAK OR
STRONG?"

Mr. Mike walks down the row of kids.
"I just want to check your bags and shoes."
What?
I put my hands over my fanny pack.
But Mr. Mike gives me a thumbs-up.
"A fanny pack is fine.
And good shoes too, Ellis."
He looks at Nick and shakes his head.
"That backpack is much too big, dude.
You'll have to leave it here."

Phew.
I'm sweating already.

Ms. Kim introduces the woman next
to her.
"Kids, this is Holly Jolly.
You probably know her from the internet."
My classmates whoop and cheer.
"I love you, Holly!" Fay shrieks.

I've never heard of Holly Jolly.

"Holly is famous," says Ms. Kim.
"She has almost a million followers.
And she knows all about healthy eating.
She thinks our school is fantastic.
Our HEALTHY School.
Today she's come to film us.
And we're super proud.
That is SO terrific, Holly.
SO great!"

A minute later
we're running
across a bridge.
Into the woods.

We have to run across tree trunks.
And then cross the water by hanging
from ropes.
I'm scared to death that I'll fall in.
I have no idea whether Bob can swim
or not.
He's jabbing me in the belly.

The group keeps running.
Ziggy is in the lead.
Ms. Kim is behind him.
Holly Jolly darts around them.
Just like an orange butterfly.

I slow down and Dante notices.
He wipes some mud off his face.
"Boy, this sure is fun," he says.
"You okay?"
Bob sticks his head out of my fanny pack.

This is awful!

Bob unzips my pack a little further.

He jumps out.

"What on earth are you doing!" I yell.

I look around.

But we're alone.

"Do you want to join in?" Dante asks Bob.

"Till we're within sight of the others?

No one can see you here."

Bob stretches and does a couple of knee bends.

"That's a better idea.

What are you waiting for?

I'm ready to go."

CHAPTER 18

DON'T GET MAD, BOB!

We run through the woods.
Dante, Bob, and me.
This is really fun!
Dante runs super fast.
He keeps waiting for us to catch up.
"Just keep going," I shout.
"We'll get there on our own."
I see Dante hesitate.
But then he sticks up his thumb.
And sprints further.

This is great.
Just me and Bob.
He really cracks me up.
Finally I can laugh out loud.

But suddenly I see someone behind me.
It's the man with the goatee again!
I grab Bob and run away as fast as I can.

I run as fast as the wind.

Then I fall into a ditch.

I sink down, deeper and deeper.
Up to my belly button.
The mud is pulling me in.
It's weirdly cold.
And it stinks!
Bob climbs onto my head.
Luckily I stop sinking.
But I can't move either.

The man with the goatee walks up to me.
I glare at him.
He sticks out his arms.
But Bob is *just* out of reach.
"Go away!" I scream.
"Buzz off!" hollers Bob.
He's trembling all over.
Oh, no.
"DON'T GET MAD, BOB!" I shout.

But it's too late.
Bob is furious.
He explodes.

Right into the man's arms.

CHAPTER 19

KIDNAPPED

I scream and shout.
But the man with the goatee runs away.
With Bob in his hands.
"BOB!" I call.
My voice sounds hoarse.
This is like a nightmare.
Where you have to run, but you're stuck.
Where you want to scream, but your voice
is gone.
Suddenly I see Dante in the distance.
He comes running up to me.
"He…has…Bob!" I stammer.

Dante grabs a branch and holds it out
to me.
He pulls me out of the ditch.
Then we run like crazy through the woods.
Spattering mud everywhere.
In the distance we see the man.
He runs down to the water.
Then he jumps on a raft and pushes off
with a stick.

I point to a canoe.
One second later and we're inside it.

We paddle like a machine.
"Ellis and Dante!" I suddenly hear.
It's Ms. Kim.
We paddle past the class.
Hasna waves.
The teacher looks at us with her mouth
hanging open.
Holly Jolly films it all.

We wave back.
"Ms. Kim!" Dante shouts.
"Look how fast we're going.
We're taking another route!"

The man on the raft goes fast too.
Much too fast.
We're still in the middle of the lake.
But he's already on the other side.
He jumps onto the shore.
A woman from the sports club is standing
there.

She looks strong.
With one hand, she holds the man back.

With her other hand, she raises a
megaphone to her mouth.

"YESSS!" she shouts.

Her voice booms across the water.

"We have a WINNER!"

I look around.

My class is on the other side of the lake.

Some of the kids are already running onto
the bridge.

The woman grabs the man's arm and
raises it.

She asks him something.

"His name is BILL!" she shouts.

"Mr. Bill has won the first prize!
Won't your class be proud!"

But Bill breaks loose and runs to his bike.
"Don't let him go!" I scream.
"He's not our teacher!"
"WHAT?" cries the woman.
"He's a thief!" I shout.
We tie our canoe up on the shore.
I jump out and race past the woman with the megaphone.
The man called Bill has already biked away.
Dante runs after me, across the grass.
"There!" I shout.
We jump into a big go-kart.
And we pedal after the man.

We pedal like crazy.
But it's hopeless.
We can barely see the man anymore.
He's just a dot in the distance.
Without saying a word, we turn around.

Ms. Kim is waiting for us.
She looks very angry.
"What made you think you could just grab
a canoe like that?" she scolds.
But I don't listen to the rest.
My head is swimming.
I've got to get out of here right away—to
save Bob.
Suddenly Holly Jolly puts her hand on my
shoulder.
"Didn't this young
lady come in first?
I think she's
the winner."

The adults start talking together.
Ms. Kim is waving her arms.
But that soon changes.
Suddenly she nods her head energetically.
And she smiles at Holly Jolly.
Ziggy walks up to me.
"Congratulations!
You're the WINNER!"
He hangs a gold medal around my neck.
It sticks to my shirt.
I look at Dante.
He knows I'm not the winner.
I'm the biggest loser ever.
I lost Bob.

CHAPTER 20

WHOA!

Dante's mother picks us up.

"How great of you two," she says.

She drives out of the woods.

"You won first and second prize!"

Dante doesn't say a thing.

He fiddles with his silver medal.

I stare out the window.

"You must be worn out," says Dante's mother.

Just then we drive past the park.

Wait a minute, this is right near Bill's hotel!

"STOP!" I shout.

Dante's mother slams on the brakes.

"What's wrong?"

Dante knows right away what's wrong.
"Ellis left something in the park, Mom.
We should go and look for it.
Then we'll walk back home, okay?"
"Ah, Ellis," says his mother.

It's not your cute little stuffed popcorn, is it?

I swallow.
"Yes, it is," I mumble.

Soon we're running through the park to
the hotel.
The bike is leaning against the wall.
The bike that took Bob away.
"He's here," I whisper.
"But how do we get inside?"
"Through the door," says Dante.
"Get real," I say.
"Have you seen yourself?"

But Dante is already walking up to the
entrance.
"Maybe they won't pay any attention
to us."

Well, they *do* pay attention to us.
"Hey, you two!"
The man behind the desk jumps to
his feet.
He runs up to us.
And he waves us out the door.

What do you
think you're doing?

"This hotel is only for guests.
It is not a playground.
Go on, scram!"

"We'll go around back," says Dante.
He drags me along, around the corner.
We walk through a little gate.
Where we see a kind of courtyard and two big doors.
Both of them are open.
I just walk right in.
"Whoa, little girl!" I hear someone shout.

What are you doing here?

It's a cook, you can tell.
He points at me with a leek.
"You can't come in here."

"We've come for an interview," I blurt out.
"We're from the healthy school.
Can we ask you some questions?"
Dante nods his head up and down.
"For our school report."
The cook looks doubtful.
He scowls at us.
"With such filthy hands?" he asks.
"And such dirty faces?"
He points to a counter.
"Wash.
With hot water
and soap.
Then you can
ask questions."
He points
to a pot.
"I'm working
on the soup."

We go over to the counter.

"Where do we go from here?" Dante whispers.

"Maybe that way," I say.

I point to a door.

We tiptoe over and push it open.

"Whoa," we hear behind us.

We run up the stairs as fast as we can.

CHAPTER 21

BOY OH BOY

We sneak through the corridors of
the hotel.
Up and up, floor by floor.
I look around, listening at the doors.
No sign of Bob.
No sign of anybody.
How are we ever going to find him?
But on the seventh floor I see something.
Muddy footsteps.
They lead from the elevator into one of
the corridors.
We follow the tracks.
And end up at a door.

We press our ears against the
smooth wood.
My heart skips a beat.
"Do you hear that?" I ask.
"Bob," Dante whispers.

Sounds to me like he's laughing.

We look at each other with surprise.
Then I hear a grumbly voice.
"It's that man, Bill," I whisper.
"Can you understand what he's saying?"
"Let me listen," says Dante.

"He's being really nice to
Bob," says Dante.
"He's talking about how great
it is that he's so big.
And that he can explode
so well.
I don't think Bob can
understand a word.
But he thinks he's funny."
Dante goes on listening.
"That guy thinks Bob is really
terrific."
"What a SLIMEBALL," I say.
Just a little too loud.
Suddenly everything goes quiet
inside.
Then the door slowly opens
a crack.
I'm looking straight into the
eyes of Bill.

He tries to shut the door again.
But I stick my foot in the doorway.
"Bob?" I call into the room.
"Ellis?" I hear.
And then the familiar pitter-patter of
popcorn kernel feet.
I push the door open.

I want to say how glad I am.
That I missed him so much.
That I never, ever want to lose him again.
But instead of that I say:

Why didn't you bite
that man on the nose?

"He gave me food," Bob answers.
"HE KIDNAPPED YOU!" I scream.
"Boy oh boy," Bob mutters.
"Maybe you should count to ten."

The man sits down on the bed.
He points to his chest.
"Bill," he says.
He takes off his hat.
Suddenly he doesn't look so mean.
He starts to talk.
About America.
About Coraline Corn, his boss.
Dante translates it all into Dutch.
This Coraline Corn wants to get her hands
on Bob.
Bill has to arrange it.
He can't go home until he does.

Soon I know
everything.

About Bill's popcorn farm.

About the illegal growth tonic.

About his super-tall
corn plants.

Soon I'll be rich!

That the popcorn kernels *didn't* pop.

And that Bill sold them to Coraline's factory *anyway*.

Now he's really sorry.
He doesn't want to give Bob to Coraline.
I know that now too.
But I can't believe what we're going
to do next.

CHAPTER 22

QUIT YOUR YAPPING, LADY

We all get into the elevator.
And take it to the highest floor in the hotel.
I'm holding Bob.

Can I push the button?

I look at Bill
from the corner
of my eye.
That man has been
following us for days.
He kidnapped Bob.
And now we're going to
help him!

Bob laughs at himself
in the mirror.

I look like a swamp creature.
The ride doesn't take very long.
"PING!" says the elevator.
The doors whish open.
It feels like we're
walking out of
a microwave.

We walk out into a little hallway.
There's only one door.
A very big one.
I see a camera with a doorbell under it.
"I don't like the look of this," I say.
I tuck Bob into my fanny pack.

And zip it up.
Bill rings the
doorbell.
A woman opens
the door.
I recognize her
right away.
So this is Coraline.
She looks from Bill
to Dante with piercing eyes.

And then she
looks at me.
I feel a shiver run
down my spine.

"So, here we are," I say.
And we walk in.

The woman talks to Bill.
He laughs a sarcastic sort of laugh.
I'm beginning to wonder what's going on.
Are we being lured into a trap?
Dante gives me a poke.
Yeah, yeah, I'll do what we agreed on.
I unzip my fanny pack.
And take Bob out.

Bob is lying limp in my hand.
With his eyes closed.
The woman frowns and says something.
"She wants to know if he's dead," Dante
translates.
I nod.
"Dead as a doornail," I say.
I shake my hand a little.
Bob rocks back and forth.
He does it so well it's just plain scary.
"So, problem solved," I say.
"No more live popcorn kernel.
You can go back to America."
I know very well that she doesn't
understand me.
But hopefully she gets it anyway.
I take a deep breath and look her straight
in the eye.

Suddenly the woman steps forward.
She snatches Bob out of my hand.
"Ugh," he sputters.

Don't pinch like that, you crazy woman!

"AHA!" shouts
Coraline.
She starts
talking very fast.
Dante translates
quietly.
"She's taking
him with her to
America.
She says that,
uh…"
Dante's
mouth falls
open.

"Ellis, she says there are MORE of them.

MORE LIVE POPCORN KERNELS!

They're someplace where they can't do
any harm.
Bob has to go there too, she says.
For our own safety."

Bob struggles to free himself.

QUIT YOUR YAPPING, LADY!

Bob turns bright yellow.
He starts shaking and
trembling.
He changes into a big
piece of popcorn.
But *before* he goes
bouncing around
the room...
He first bites Coraline
on the nose.

CHAPTER 23

MMM!

Farmer Bill winks at me.
He runs up to Bob.
I see him hide Bob in his shirt.
But he also starts to chew.
His jaws grind up and down.
He makes very loud
smacking sounds.
Then he wipes his
mouth.
Coraline stares at him.
"She wants to know if
he's really eaten him,"
Dante translates.
Bill gives him a thumbs-up.
"Mmm."
"He says, mmm," says Dante.
"Yes," I say, very confused.
"*That* I understood."

Coraline carries on for quite some time.
She really thinks Bill has eaten Bob.
She walks around the room in circles.
And she talks to herself.
As if we weren't there.
"Stupid farmer," Dante translates.
"That wasn't what was supposed
to happen.
But anyway, at least I'm rid of him."

Coraline straightens her back.
She walks to the door with
long strides and opens it.

"We have to leave," says Dante.
"Tomorrow she and Bill are going home."

Bill, Dante, and I rush to the elevator.
Bill takes Bob out from under his shirt.
We cheer quietly.
"Well done, Bob," I say.
But Bob doesn't look so happy.
"Are you okay?" I ask.
Dante looks worried.
"What's wrong with him?"

Uh-oh.

"To the kitchen," I say quickly.
"We have to go back to the kitchen."
"Do you want to push the button?"
I ask Bob.
But he doesn't say a word.
This is really not good.
"Hurry up, hurry up," I say to the elevator.

Dante and Bill go on ahead.
People with white aprons come up to us.
"You again?" I hear them say.
Dante and Bill speak to the cooks.
I look for a microwave.
And quickly put Bob inside.

It only takes a minute.
But it feels like a year.
Dante and Bill keep everyone in the
kitchen distracted.
But it works!
Bob comes out of the microwave as good
as new.
"Let's get out of here," I whisper.
We run outside.
Once we're around the corner we stop.
"Now we can finally go home," I say.
"No," says Bob.

I want to go to America.

CHAPTER 24

BYE!

The next day, Holly Jolly is at school.

We're going to watch her movie.

Everyone is waiting in the auditorium.

Ms. Kim is on the stage.

Holly Jolly is standing next to her.

"Dear children," Ms. Kim says.

"You are all so fantastic!

Everybody did so well at field day yesterday.

And you can just FEEL that this school has only healthy food and drinks."

"It wasn't easy for everyone," she goes on.
She looks at me.
"Some children really had to figure
things out.
I'm extra proud of you, Ellis.
It's so amazing how much you've
changed!
And then winning the contest too.
Well done."

I smile, but just a little.
"Are you kidding?" someone calls out.
"This really isn't fair!"
Fay stands up.
She walks to the stage.

Fay points at me.
"She ALWAYS takes popcorn to school!
And she passes it out to the whole class!"
I look at Dante.

Weren't you going to draw
a unicorn for her?

He rubs his nose.
"Oops," he says.
"Forgot."
Ms. Kim turns bright red.
"ELLIS!"
But then Holly Jolly starts clapping
her hands.

Oh, popcorn, that's FANTASTIC!

Holly Jolly licks her lips.
"Popcorn is the best
snack ever.
Light and airy.
I eat it almost every day.
It's absolutely
harmless.
Healthy eating can be
fun too.
Right, Kim?"
Ms. Kim stares at her.
"How clever of Ellis," Holly Jolly
continues.
"I can understand why you're so proud
of her."
Ms. Kim blinks her eyes.
"Uh...I, uh," she stutters.
"Well, yes, Holly, when you put it
THAT way."

Who would have thought?
Popcorn is no longer forbidden.
We can eat it at school again.
Thanks to Holly Jolly.
Now I don't have to sneak it anymore.
It's great.
Really great.
But I don't feel relieved.
I keep thinking about Bob.
He wants to go to America.

After school we go to the park.
We've agreed to meet Bill under the tree.
He's already there.
Bob gives him a fist bump.

Billy!

Then he does a handstand.
"I've thought a lot about it," I say.
"But I don't want
you to leave, Bob."

Bob rolls over.

Who said anything about LEAVING?

You're coming with me, right?

"How can I do
THAT?" I ask.
"I have my fathers.
And school.
I can't just fly to America."
Then Bill says something.
"He wants to help," says Dante.
"To make up for what he's done."

I don't have to tell Bill where I live.
He already knows.
We wait for him in the park.

It takes a really long time.
But finally I see something.
Bill is biking toward us, swaying from side
to side.
The three of us stand there together.
"And?" I call out to Bill.
"Did you talk to my fathers?"
Bill gives us a thumbs-up.

It's Friday.
We're sitting in my popcorn paradise.
I'm making three bags of popcorn.
One for Bob.
One for Dante.
And one for me.
I don't know *how* Bill did it, but suddenly
my fathers want to go to America.
For their work.
We're going there this summer.
And Dante can come along!
Only a few more weeks of school.
Bob is already practicing his English.
"AMERICA…HERE WE COME!" he
shouts in English.

THE END*

*Well, not really…

THE ORIGINAL

 POPCORN BOB

BOOK 1

ALSO AVAILABLE

HUNGRY FOR MORE
☆ POPCORN BOB? ☆

BOOK 3

COMING SOON